red blue
cat cat

This book is dedicated to my sister and brother, Gabby and Dom—
J.D.

Copyright © 2012 by Jenni Desmond
All rights reserved/CIP data is available.
Published in the United States 2012 by
Blue Apple Books, 515 Valley Street,
Maplewood, NJ 07040
www.blueapplebooks.com
First Edition
Printed in China 09/12
ISBN: 978-1-60905-248-5
1 3 5 7 9 10 8 6 4 2

BLUE 🍎 APPLE

Red Cat and **Blue Cat** lived in the same house.

Blue Cat
stayed upstairs.

Red Cat stayed downstairs.

Whenever they saw each other—

it was NOT good. Not good at all.

But neither cat knew about the other's secret wish.

Red Cat wished he were
as smart as **Blue Cat**, and . . .

Blue Cat wanted to be
fast and bouncy
like **Red Cat**.

So they fought and they hissed
and they wished, all day long.

One day, **Blue Cat** had a good idea.

"If I turn myself red, I will become fast and bouncy!" he said.

So he ate a crab . . .

some cherries . . .

a watermelon . . .

strawberries . . .

and rose petals.

Guess who was spying on
him the whole time?

"I will show Blue Cat who's smart!" said **Red Cat.**

He ate blueberries . . .

bluebells . . .

a blue fish . . .

blue pudding . . .

and certain cupcakes.

It did NOT work.
Not at all!

Blue Cat
stayed blue

and **Red Cat**
stayed red.

And both cats were a bit sad and a bit angry.

"I will try
something different,"
declared **Blue Cat.**

"Look at me!
I'm red!"
he said.

Red Cat came up with his own plan.
"If I roll in this blue paint, I will become a blue cat!" he said.

tip

splatter

Red Cat went to show **Blue Cat**
his brand new self.

"I'm blue, too!"
said **Red Cat**.

"I'm a red cat!"
said **Blue Cat**.

It had not worked. Not at all.

"Are you trying to be like me?"
asked **Blue Cat**.

"Maybe," said **Red Cat**.
"But I am too sticky."

"And I am too hot,"
Blue Cat admitted.

-tug-

Both cats helped each other become un-red and not-blue.

pull

Red Cat helped Blue Cat take off his red clothes.

Blue Cat washed Red Cat's hard-to-clean paint spots.

rub-a-scrub

But they were not done yet. Not even close.

"Here's what you need to do to be exactly like me," said **Blue Cat.**

He showed **Red Cat** how to come up with smart ideas.

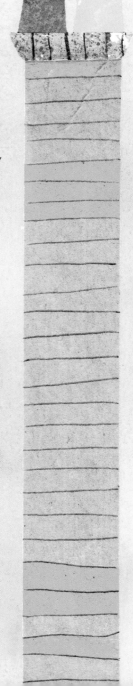

boing

"Don't you want to be like me?" asked **Red Cat**.

"Well, maybe," said **Blue Cat**, "just a little bit."

Red Cat showed
Blue Cat how to run
fast and jump high.

"Follow me!"
said Red Cat.

boing

boing

Each worked hard—

very hard —

to be exactly like the other.

But something was not quite right.

"I think I like being **Red Cat** best,"
Red Cat admitted.

"I can't run as fast as you," said **Blue Cat**.
"But I am the best **Blue Cat** ever."

They were still
Blue Cat and **Red Cat**.

But something HAD changed.

Red Cat and **Blue Cat** were friends!
They did all sorts of fast, bouncy,
and clever things—together!

Then, one day . . .

Miaw

meeaaaw

they spotted **Yellow Cat!**

"Can you sing?"
asked **Red Cat.**

"Should we be yellow?"
asked **Blue Cat.**

Here we go again!